Building Site
Activity Fun

Copy the picture of the big digger. It's easy if you do it square by square. Now colour your picture, and write your name on the line.

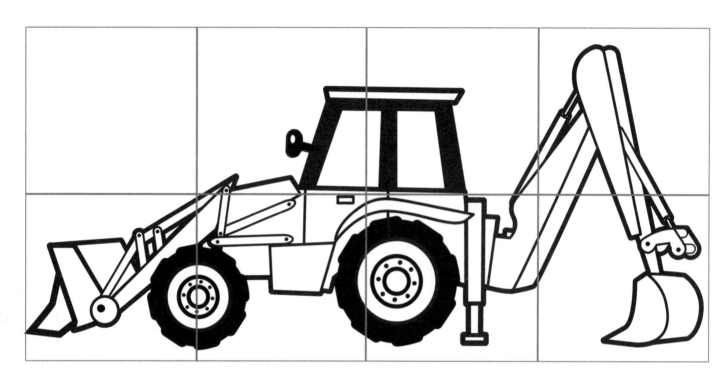

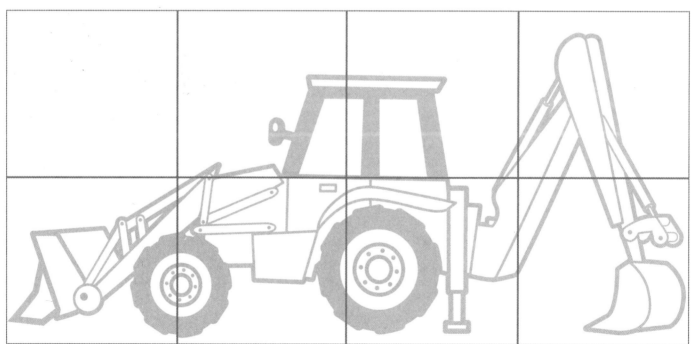

My digger picture, by _____

These digger pictures look the same, but 5 things are different in picture 2.
Can you spot all 5 differences?

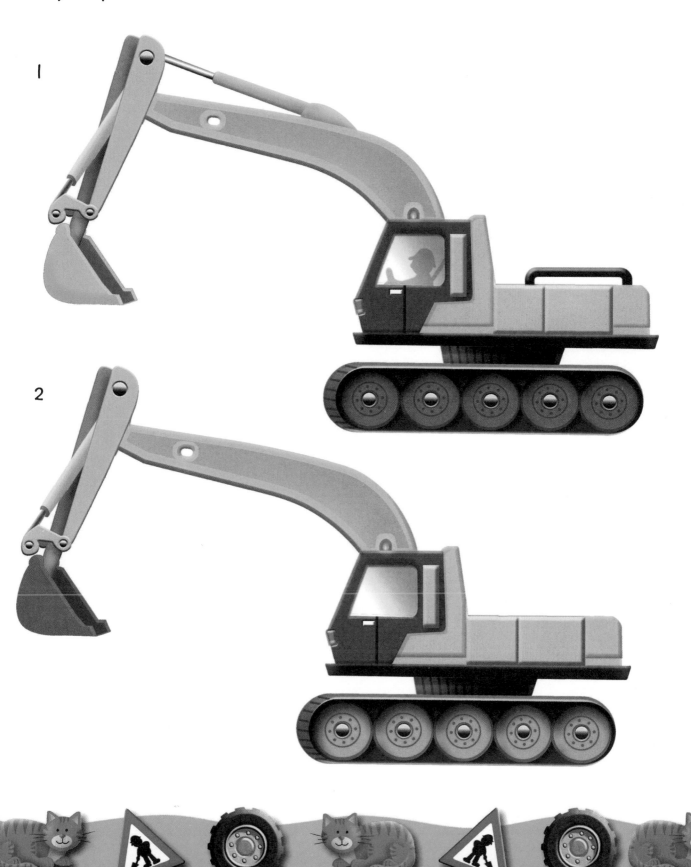

1

2

The dumper has knocked over lots of tins of paint. Colour the paint spills to match the lids.

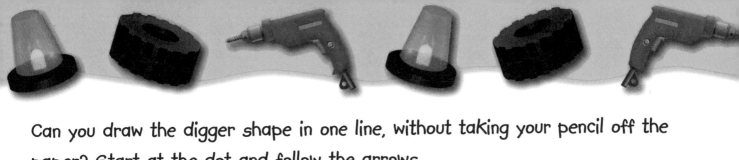

Can you draw the digger shape in one line, without taking your pencil off the paper? Start at the dot and follow the arrows.

Can you draw lines to match the trucks to the diggers their tyres have made?

a 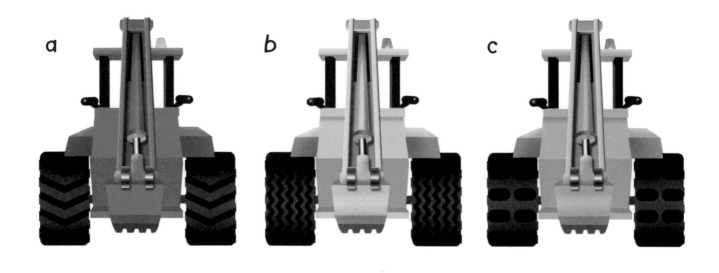 b c

1

2

3

There are 5 things here that do NOT belong on the building site.
Can you find and colour them?

Answer: the pirates hat, toothbrush, balloon, sheep and teddy bear.

There are 6 spare tyres hidden on the building site. Can you find them all?

Can you draw more tyre patterns to fill the page?

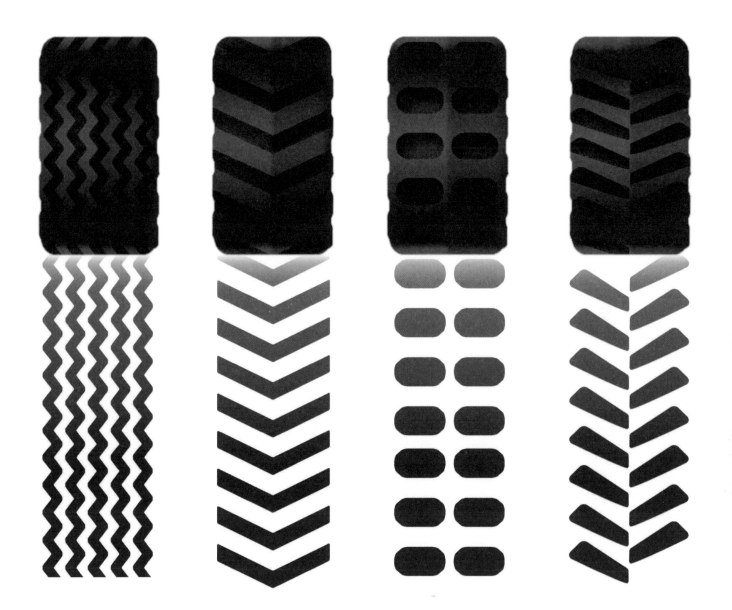

Starting at number 1, join the dots to find out what this big machine is.

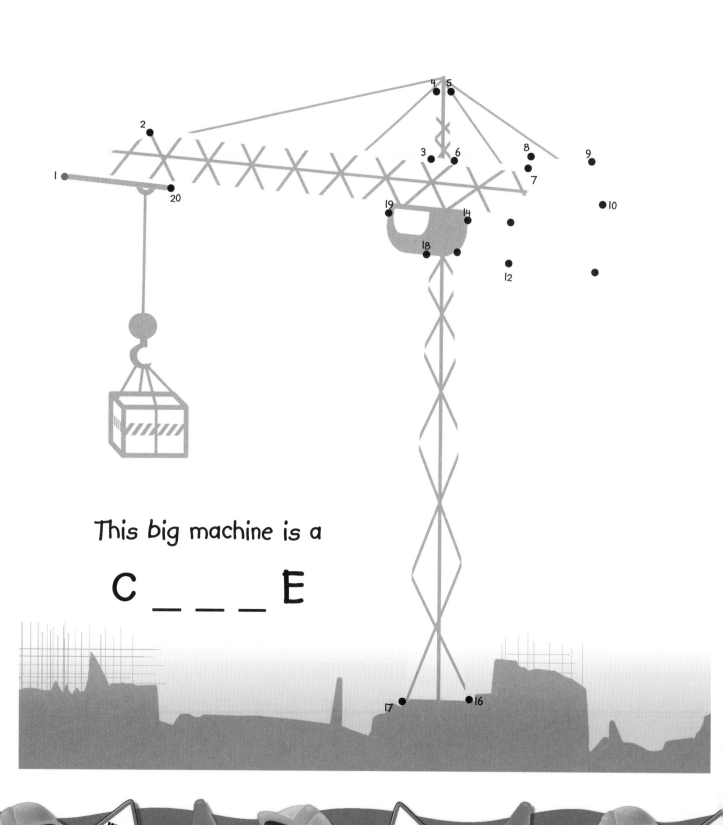

This big machine is a

C _ _ _ E

These bulldozers look the same, but one is different.
Find the odd one out and circle it.

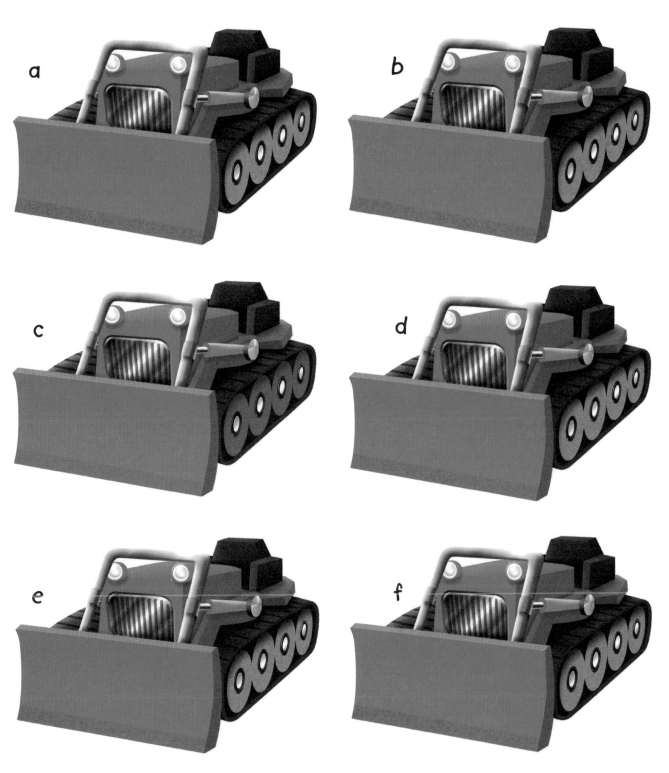

Can you draw the dumper outline, without lifting your pencil from the paper? Start at the dot and follow the arrows. Why not draw wheels and a cab to complete your drawing?

How many wheels are there on this page? Don't forget to count the ones you can't see!

DD 1

Answer: there are 11 wheels in this page.

Count the tools, and write the number for each set in the box underneath.

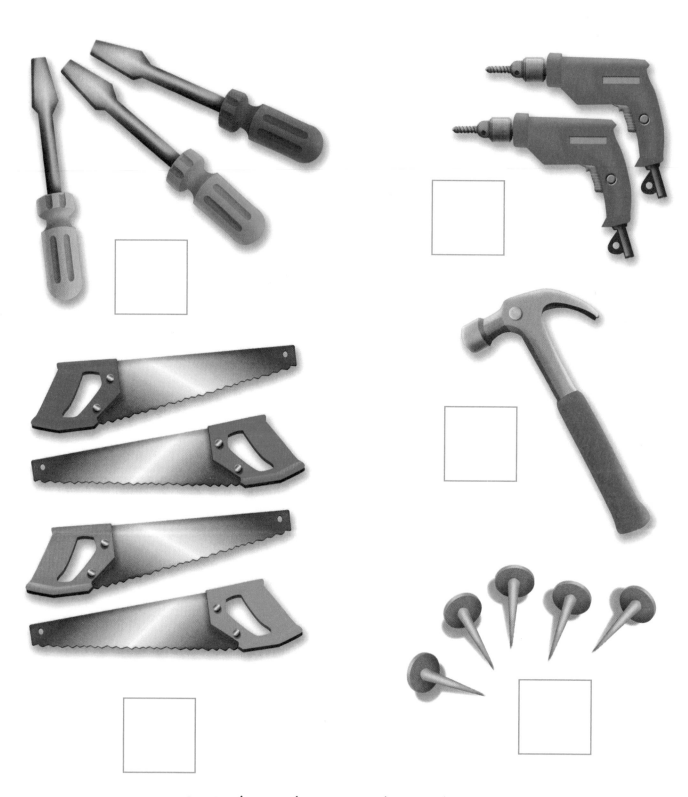

Which jigsaw piece will complete the picture? Draw a circle around it.

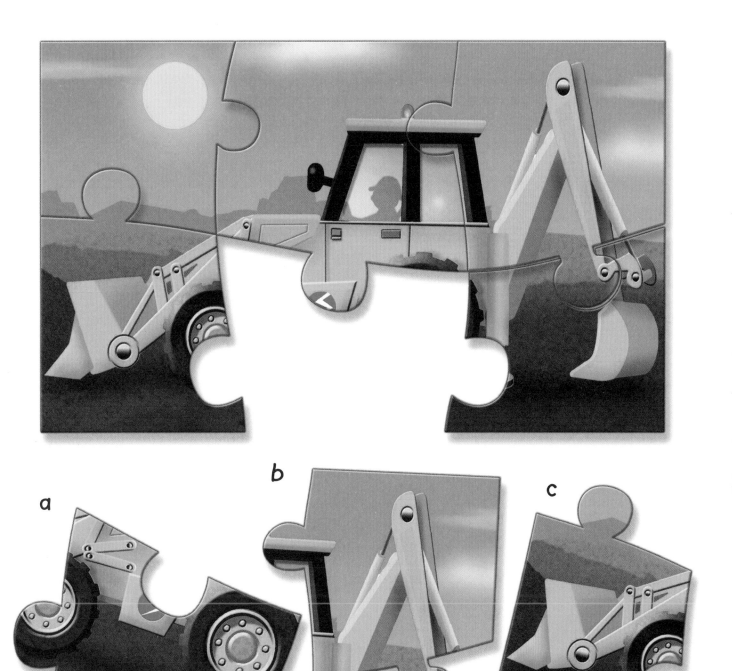

a

b

c

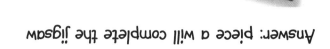

These tools look the same, but 1 is different in each set. Can you circle the odd ones out?

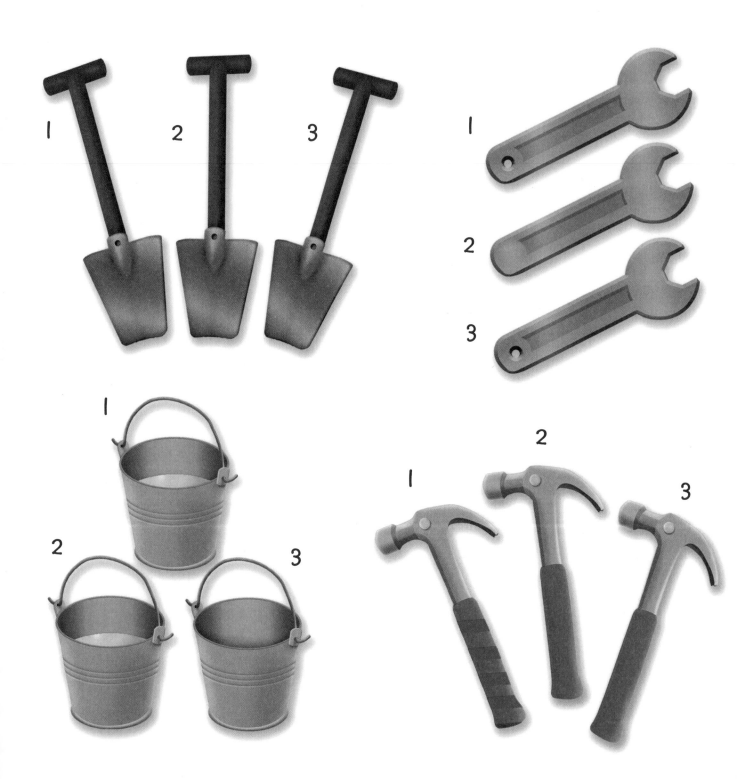

Which of these details can you see in the big picture?

Write a tick (✓) for yes or a cross (x) for no.

Copy the picture of the steam roller. Draw it square by square, then colour it using the small picture as a guide.

The workers can't go on to the site without their hard hats.
Can you find a hard hat for each worker? Colour each one yellow.

Colour only the shapes with a blue spot in them. What can you see?

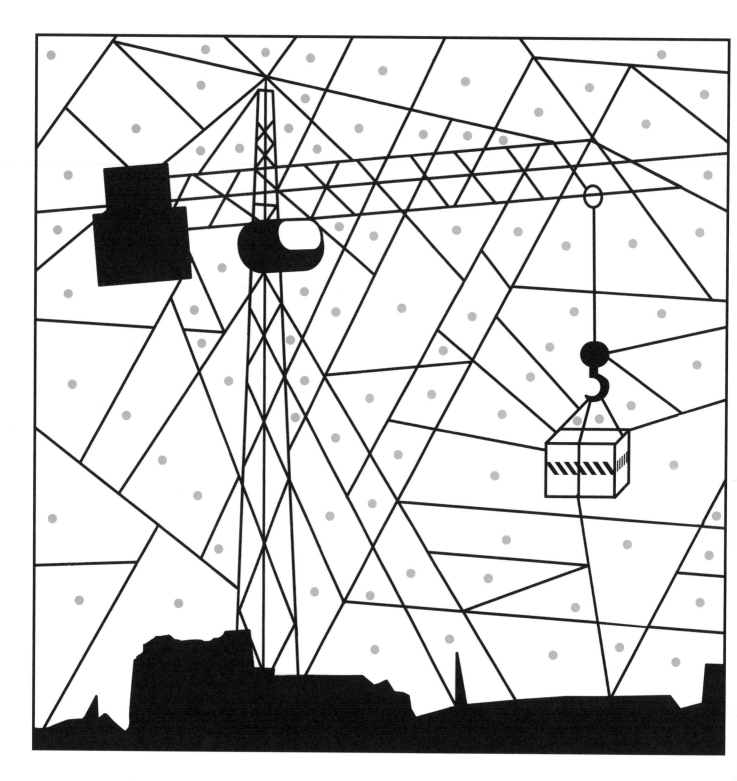

Answer: it's a crane.

Can you show the dumper the way to the truck without crossing any barriers?

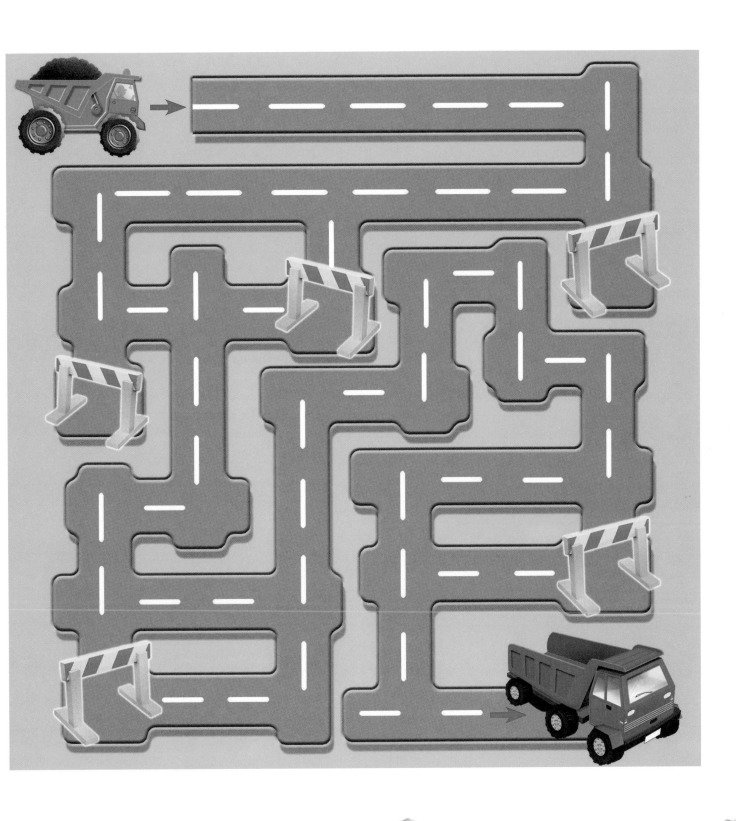

These trucks look the same, but one is different. Which is the odd one out, and why?

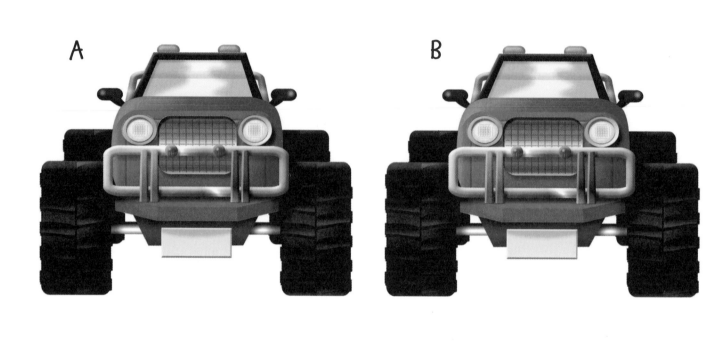

A

B

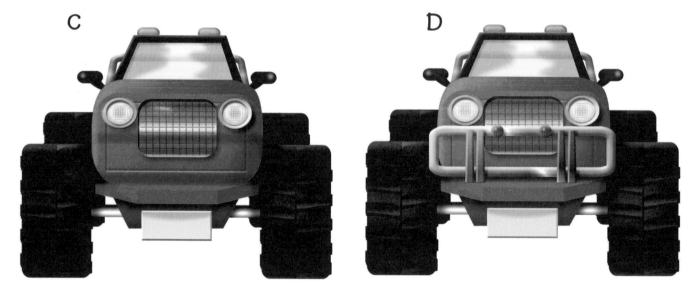

C

D

Answer: truck C is the odd one out.

Colour in the picture as neatly as you can, and write your name on the tyre.

It's the end of a busy day, and the diggers and dumpers are quiet – until tomorrow. Colour in the picture, before you say goodnight.